STILL STUCK

SHINSUKE YOSHITAKE

ABRAMS BOOKS FOR YOUNG READERS, NEW YORK

It all started when Mom said it was time for a bath.

She wanted to help me get ready, but I told her I could do it all by myself.

I tried and tried to get my shirt off.

But I was stuck.

What would happen if I was stuck forever?

I was sure lots of important people had been stuck before.

I couldn't have been the first.

Maybe I didn't need to get unstuck?

It wouldn't be so bad . . .

I would find a way.

But what if the cat tickled my tummy?

How would I make him stop?

I bet we would have fun together.

So I decided to stay that way forever! It wasn't so bad.

But then I got cold. I thought about asking Mom for help . . .

No! I could do it myself!

Maybe it would help if I took my pants off first?

Uh-oh.

That was a bad idea.

KNOCK-KNOCK.

SCRUB-SCRUB.

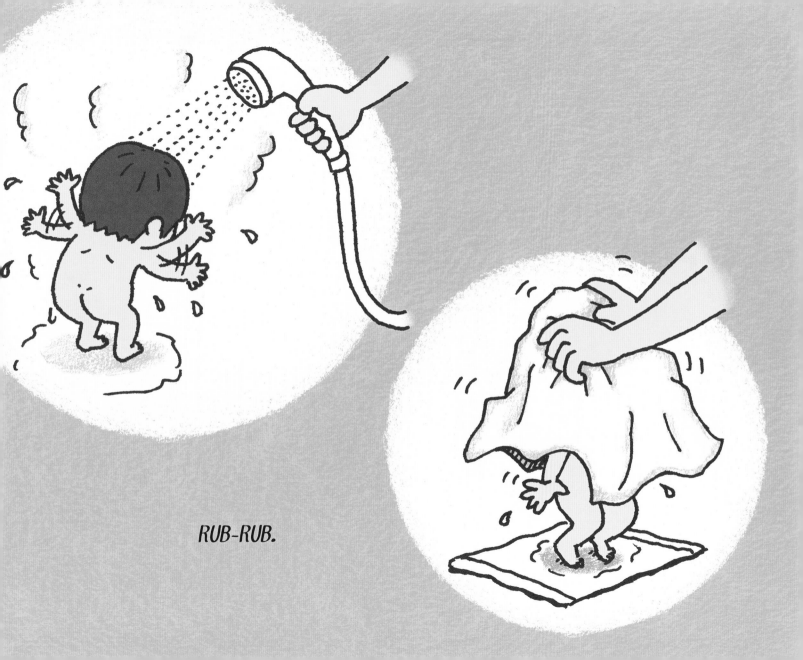

RUB-RUB.

Now, Mom says it's time to put on my pajamas.

First I put on my underwear.

Then I put on my pants.

I knew I could do it by myself!

Until . . .

I'm stuck . . . *again.*